rain Brings

by Maryann Cocca-Leffler

Frogs

A Little Book of HOPE

HARPER
An Imprint of HarperCollinsPublishers

Rain Brings Frogs

Copyright © 2011 by Maryann Cocca-Leffler

All rights reserved. Printed in the United States of America.

No part of this book may be used or reproduced in any manner whatsoever without written permission except in the case of brief quotations embodied in critical articles and reviews. For information address HarperCollins Children's Books, a division of HarperCollins Publishers, 10 East 53rd Street, New York, NY 10022.

www.harpercollinschildrens.com

Library of Congress Cataloging-in-Publication Data is available.

ISBN 978-0-06-196106-9

Typography by Joe Merkel

11 12 13 14 15 LPR 10 9 8 7 6 5 4 3 2

❖

First Edition

To Janine,
Who always sees the bright side.
Love, Mom

When Mom says,

I Hate rain.

Nate says,

rain brings frogs!

When Ben says,

NOt enough.

Nate says,

Enough to share.

When his sister says,

It's so UGLY!

Nate says,

It's SO warm!

When Charlie says,

Nate says,

room for **ALL.**

When Dad says, mud. mUD. Mud.

Nate says,

rainbow!

rainbow!

rainbow!

rainbow!

When Casey says,

I LOST.

Nate says,

I FINISHED!

I NEED More!

Nate says,

I need one.

When his friends say,

nothing to do.

Nate says,

ENjoy the View!

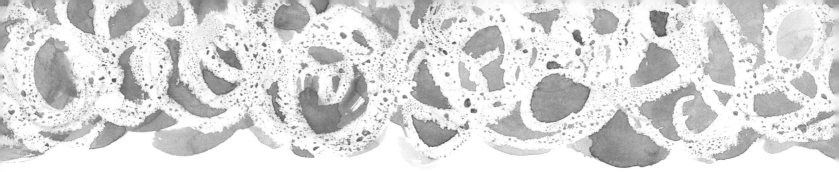

When everyone says,

we see clouds.

Nate says,

Behind the clouds...

sun!

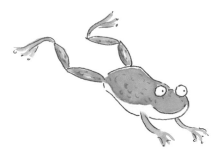

hope   hope

Maryann Cocca-Leffler is the author and illustrator of over forty-five books for children. Maryann owes both her optimistic view of life and the idea for this book to her daughter, Janine, who has always seen the bright side of any situation. Many of Maryann's other books were inspired by her family and her own childhood, including PRINCESS K.I.M. AND THE LIE THAT GREW and the award-winning MR. TANEN'S TIES and BUS ROUTE TO BOSTON. Maryann lives with her family in New Hampshire. You can visit her online at www.maryanncoccaleffler.com.

For more information on your favorite authors and artists, visit www.authortracker.com.